Ant and Honey Bee

A PAIR OF
FRIENDS AT HALLOWEEN

Megan McDonald

illustrated by G. Brian Karas

CANDLEWICK PRESS

For Judi Ingram Adkins
M. M.

For Ben and Sam
G. B. K.

Text copyright © 2005, 2010 by Megan McDonald
Illustrations copyright © 2005, 2010 by G. Brian Karas

First paperback edition in this format 2013

The Library of Congress has cataloged the hardcover edition as follows:

McDonald, Megan.
Ant and Honey Bee : a pair of friends at Halloween / Megan McDonald ; illustrated by G. Brian Karas. — 2nd ed.
p. cm.
Summary: Best friends Ant and Honey Bee, who think of themselves as quite a pair,
become matching home appliances on Halloween.
ISBN 978-0-7636-4662-2 (hardcover)
[1. Costume—Fiction. 2. Halloween—Fiction. 3. Friendship—Fiction 4. Ants—Fiction.
5. Honeybee—Fiction. 6. Bees—Fiction.] I. Karas, G. Brian, ill. II. Title.
PZ7.M478419Am 2010
[E] — dc22   2009021485

ISBN 978-0-7636-6864-8 (paperback)

13 14 15 16 17 18 SWT 10 9 8 7 6 5 4 3 2 1

Printed in Dongguan, Guangdong, China

This book was typeset in Usherwood.
The illustrations were done in gouache, acrylic, and pencil.

Candlewick Press
99 Dover Street
Somerville, Massachusetts 02144

visit us at www.candlewick.com

Contents

CHAPTER 1
Ant and Honey Bee

Ant was getting antsy.

She stared out the window. Only a few hours left till trick-or-treat.

"What can we be for trick-or-treat?" Ant asked her friend Honey Bee.

"Pilgrims," said Honey Bee.

"Pilgrims! But we've been pilgrims for two years in a row," said Ant. "Pilgrims are boring."

"Maybe," said Honey Bee. "But we already have pilgrim costumes."

"I'm sick of that ugly gray dress and apron," said Ant. "I'm sick of those itchy pilgrim socks. And I'm sick of that funny pilgrim hat. Let's be something different."

"Then be . . . an ear of corn, if it will make you happy," said Honey Bee.

"Hmm," said Ant. "An ear of corn would be different. An ear of corn would be not-boring. But what will you be if I am an ear of corn?"

"None of your beeswax," said Honey Bee. She smiled at her friend to show she was just kidding. "I'll be a bee," she said.

"But you *are* a bee!" Ant said. "You can't just be you."

"It's good to be yourself," said Honey Bee.

"You can be yourself anytime," said Ant.

"Then I will be a *queen* bee," said
Honey Bee.

"A queen bee is still a bee," said Ant.
"A big, bossy bee."

"Then I will be a bumblebee," said
Honey Bee.

"A bumblebee is still a bee. A big,
hairy bee."

"Okay, okay," said Honey Bee. "I will be a wasp. A wasp is not a bee!"

"But a wasp is almost like a bee," said Ant.

Honey Bee did not look happy.

"Isn't it?" asked Ant in a small voice.

"A wasp is not at all like a bee," said Honey Bee. "A wasp is not the teeniest tiniest wee bit like a bee. A wasp is mean and *eats* bees!"

Ant changed the subject. "I know! Let's be a pair."

"Sure," said Honey Bee, looking at her magazine. Ant was not one-hundred-percent sure that Honey Bee was listening. "You can be the stem," Honey Bee said.

"Huh?" said Ant. "The stem of what?"

"The stem of the pear," said Honey Bee. "I'll be the pear."

"Not *that* kind of pear!" said Ant. "A two-things-that-go-together kind of pair."

"Oh, I see," said Honey Bee, looking up at Ant. "Then how about this? I'll be an anteater."

"And what will I be if you are an anteater?"

"You can be an ant."

"But I—hey, too scary!" said Ant.

"Then I'll be a butterfly and you be a moth," said Honey Bee.

"A moth is as boring as a pilgrim!" said Ant. Sometimes Ant had ants in her pants. Honey Bee went back to reading *Hive* magazine.

Ant thought and thought about
things that go together.

She looked in the kitchen. Bacon
and eggs? Peanut butter and jelly?

She looked in the bathroom. Brush
and comb? Toilet paper and toilet?

She looked in every room of the
house. She even looked in the closet.
Sock and shoe?

Pencil and eraser?

Mop and bucket?

Movie and popcorn?

She looked in the laundry room. At last, Ant thought of the perfect pair.

CHAPTER 2
Washer and Dryer

Ant could not wait to tell her friend.

"Honey Bee! Honey Bee!" cried Ant. "I have the best idea. Let's be a washer and dryer!"

"A washer and dryer is as good a pair as any," said Honey Bee.

"Can I be the washer?" asked Ant.

"If I can be the dryer," said Honey Bee.

"Yippee! No more pilgrims!" cried Ant.

Ant was happier than an ear of corn.

Honey Bee was . . . well, Honey Bee would have been just as happy being a pilgrim. But if Ant was happy, Honey Bee was happy, too.

"Hurry up! Let's get started," said Ant.

Ant and Honey Bee found two boxes that were just the right size.

Ant cut lots of holes for legs and one giant hole for her head in the first box. She glued a door on top where the dirty wash goes in.

Next, Ant drew knobs that said WASH, RINSE, and SPIN.

Then she made soapsuds out of toilet paper. She glued the toilet-paper suds up and down the front of her washer.

In the other box, Honey Bee cut out holes for her legs and her wings.

She cut one big hole for her head. She glued a door to the front where the wet wash goes in. Honey Bee drew dials that said AIR DRY, TUMBLE DRY, and SUPER DRY.

Honey Bee glued fuzzy cotton balls for lint on her dryer.

"You're very quiet," said Ant.

"I'm busy," said Honey Bee.

"Busy as a bee?" Ant asked, smiling.

"Yes," said Honey Bee. "A good worker bee does not sit around eating royal jelly all day."

"I'm a good worker bee, too," said Ant. She went back to her washer.

They worked as hard as two ants in an anthill. They worked as hard as two bees in a beehive.

"Perfect!" said Ant.

"Perfect!" said Honey Bee.

"Wait till everyone sees us," said Ant. "We'll be the toast of the town."

"The belles of the ball," said Honey Bee.

"The cat's pajamas!" said Ant. "Nobody will have costumes like us. We dare to be different."

"Unique," said Honey Bee, puffing herself up.

"And special," said Ant. "Because we made them ourselves."

"I bet we'll get tons of treats and no tricks," said Honey Bee.

"Mountains of candy," said Ant, dreaming.

"Mmm. Gobs and gobs of Honey Drops," said Honey Bee, rubbing her tummy.

"Now let's get some clothes dirty!" said Ant. "For my washer."

Ant squirted ketchup and spilled grape juice on her pilgrim dress.

"And let's get some clothes wet," said Honey Bee. "For my dryer."

Honey Bee dunked her pilgrim dress in the bathtub.

"This is very not-boring!" said Ant.

"You forgot suds!" said Honey Bee. "How can you be a washer without soapsuds?"

Ant ran to get her jar of bubble stuff. She blew some bubbles. "Blub, blub," said Ant, just like a washer when it washes clothes.

"Let me blow some bubbles," said Honey Bee.

"You can't," said Ant.

"Why not?" asked Honey Bee.

"Because you're a dryer. Dryers don't make bubbles."

"Oh," said Honey Bee. "Dryers are boring."

"But dryers go *buzz buzz* when the clothes are all dry," said Ant, trying to perk up her friend.

"Buzzing is something I can do very well!" said Honey Bee.

"**BuZzzzzz!**"

she said, just like a dryer when it's done drying.

"We make the best washer and dryer!" said Ant.

"We make the best pair!" said Honey Bee.

CHAPTER 3
Trick-or-Treat

At last it was time for trick-or-treat.
When Ant tried to walk down the front
steps, she could hardly move her legs.
When Honey Bee tried to walk down
the sidewalk, she could not see where
she was going.

"It's hard to walk when you're a
washer," said Ant.

"It's hard to see when you're a dryer,"
said Honey Bee.

The wind blew Ant and Honey Bee down the street, where they bumped into Beetle and Fly.

"Look! A pair of dice!" said Beetle.

"Very different," said Fly.

"Blub! Blub!" said Ant, so that everyone would know she was a washer.

"Buzzz," said Honey Bee, so that everyone would know she was a dryer.

"Look! Two chunks of Swiss cheese!" called Butterfly.

"Yum, yum! Are those moth holes?" asked Moth.

"Show them your spin cycle, Ant," said Honey Bee.

Ant spun around in circles "Blub! Blub!"

"Show them your tumble dry," said Ant.

Honey Bee bounced up and down.

"Buzzz!"

They spun and bounced down the hill, where they knocked on Mrs. Snail's door.

"Trick-or-treat!" yelled Ant and Honey Bee.

"Oh, a couple of ice cubes," said Mrs. Snail. "How original!" She gave them each one puny box of raisins.

"Yuck! Raisins!" said Ant.

"No Honey Drops," said Honey Bee. "And no one knows what we are."

"Mrs. Snail thought we were original," said Ant.

"No, she thought ice cubes were original."

"Next time I'll blow bubbles," said Ant, "so they'll know I'm a washer."

"Next time I'll go *buzz buzz*," said
Honey Bee, "so they'll know I'm a dryer."

Ant and Honey Bee blub-blubbed and
buzz-buzzed farther down the hill to
the Spiders' house.

"Trick-or-treat!" they yelled.

"Look! It's a stove and a dishwasher!"
said Old Man Spider.

"No, honey," said Mrs. Spider.
"Can't you see? It's a pair of computers."

"Dancing computers. Very clever!"
said Old Man Spider.

Then the Spiders gave them each one
puny sour ball.

"Uck! One puny sour ball!" said Ant.

"No Honey Drops," said Honey Bee.

Ant and Honey Bee were feeling less and less like a washer and dryer.

Honey Bee groaned.

"Mr. and Mrs. Spider thought we were clever," said Ant.

"No. They thought dancing computers were clever," said Honey Bee.

Just then, a gust of wind blew up.

Then, *plip. Plip. Plip, plip, PLIP!*

"Oh, no! Rain!" cried Ant. "Run!"

"We can't run," said Honey Bee. "We can hardly walk!"

Ant and Honey Bee waddled through the pouring rain all the way to the bottom of the hill.

"My washer is leaking!" said Ant.

"My dryer is sopping wet!" said Honey Bee.

"Let's go to Cricket's house," said Honey Bee. "Maybe he'll let us in out of the rain."

At Cricket's house, Ant and Honey Bee
dragged themselves up the steps, one,
two, three, to the front door. Ant was not
going *blub, blub*. Honey Bee was not
going *buzzz*.

"We can still yell trick-or-treat," said Ant.

"But look at our costumes," said Honey Bee.

Ant and Honey Bee did not look like a washer and dryer. They did not even look like dice or Swiss cheese or ice cubes or dancing computers. They did not even look like a two-things-that-go-together pair.

They looked like soggy blobs of
wet cardboard. A couple of mud pies.

Cricket opened the door. Cricket
was holding a great big bag of . . .
Honey Drops!

"Wait. No pilgrims this year?"
he asked.

"No," said Ant.

"No," said Honey Bee.

"So what are you?"
Cricket asked.

Ant looked at Honey Bee. Honey Bee looked at Ant.

"She's a — BEEHIVE!" said Ant.

Honey Bee smiled. "And she's an ANTHILL!"

"Creative!" said Cricket. "You make a perfect pair!"